Apple Tree
Station

Apple Tree
Village

Church

School

Farmyard Tales

The Old Steam Train

Heather Amery

Illustrated by Stephen Cartwright

Adapted by Lara Bryan

Reading consultant: Alison Kelly

Find the duck on every double page.

This story is about Apple Tree Farm,

Sam,

Poppy,

Mrs. Boot,

Mr. Boot,

and a steam train.

One morning, Poppy
and Sam were playing
with Rusty.

Mrs. Boot called to them. "We're going on a trip."

"Where are we going?"
asked Poppy.

It's a
surprise.

"Are we nearly there yet?" said Sam.

Almost...

"It's the old train
station!" cried Poppy.

"But what's everyone
doing here?"

"They're cleaning the station," said Mrs. Boot.

There's lots to do.

Poppy and Sam helped
the painter.

They heard a noise.

Choo choo

"A steam train's coming!" said Poppy.

The train stopped
at the platform.

Everyone cheered.

"All aboard," said
Mr. Boot.

"He's helping the driver
today," said Mrs. Boot.

"Can you take Rusty?"
asked Mrs. Boot.

"I have one more
surprise," said Mrs. Boot.

Mrs. Boot was the train conductor!

Mrs. Boot waved the flag
and got onto the train.

The train whistled and
started to move away.

"What a fun surprise,"
said Sam.

"Now the train is running again...

...we can ride on it every weekend!" said Mrs. Boot.

Puzzles

Puzzle 1

Put the five pictures in
the right order.

A.

B.

C.

D.

E.

23

Puzzle 2

Can you spot two chimneys,
two hats and two brooms?

Puzzle 3

Can you spot five differences between these two pictures?

Puzzle 4

What are Poppy and Sam doing? Choose the right word for each picture.

A.

walking   flying   eating

B.

playing   cheering   painting

C.

running   clapping   sitting

27

Answers to puzzles
Puzzle 1

1E.

2A.

3D.

4C.

5B.

Puzzle 2

chimney

chimney

hat

broom

hat

broom

Puzzle 3

Puzzle 4

A. walking

B. playing

C. sitting

Designed by Laura Nelson
Digital manipulation by Nick Wakeford

This edition first published in 2017 by Usborne Publishing Ltd.,
Usborne House, 83-85 Saffron Hill, London EC1N 8RT, England.
www.usborne.com Copyright © 2017, 1999 Usborne Publishing Ltd.

32

USBORNE FIRST READING
Level Two Farmyard Tales

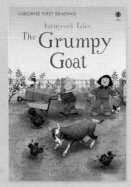

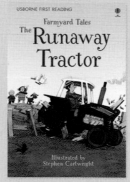

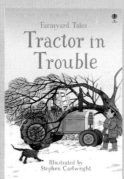

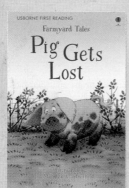

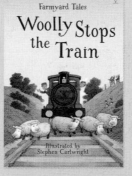

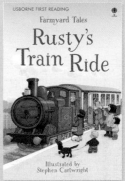